BLACKBERRY FARM

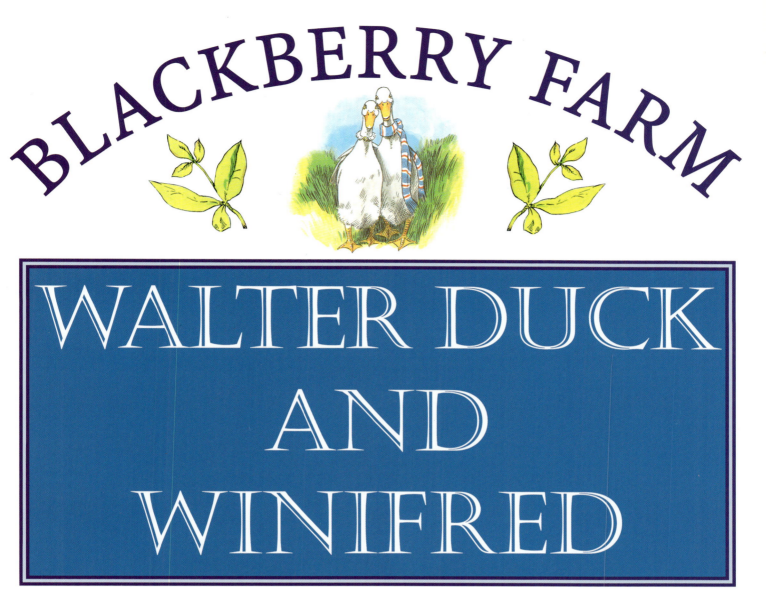

WALTER DUCK AND WINIFRED

Jane Pilgrim

WALTER DUCK AND WINIFRED

Jane Pilgrim

Illustrated by F. Stocks May

BROCKHAMPTON PRESS

Walter Duck was in quite a flutter. Joe Robin had told him that he had seen another duck, just like Walter, swimming in the river below the village near Blackberry Farm. Walter was the only duck at Blackberry Farm and sometimes he was lonely. It would be nice to have another duck to talk to.

WALTER DUCK AND WINIFRED

"Thank you for telling me, Joe," he quacked. "I think I will go and have a look." "Be careful, Walter," warned Joe. "Remember what happened last time you went up to the village." And Walter promised he would be careful. Last time he had been caught by a big black dog and had been very frightened. He did not want that to happen again.

So he sailed carefully off up the
river. dreaming as he went of a
beautiful white duck who would
come and live with him on his
part of the river.

Round the second bend of the
river he saw the lady of his
dreams and he bowed his neck to
her and said: "Good morning,
madam. My name is Walter."

"Good morning, sir," she said.
"My name is Winifred. I wonder if
you could tell me where this river
goes, as I am new to these parts?"

"Why, certainly!" said Walter. "I have just come from where it goes. It goes to Blackberry Farm. If you would like to come with me, I will show you." So Winifred and Walter sailed gracefully up the river, side by side.

When they got round the second
bend they saw Blackberry Farm
and Mr Smiles, the farmer,
standing outside with Mrs Smiles.

"It must be dinner-time," said Walter. "Would you like to stay and have dinner with me? Mr and Mrs Smiles are very kind. I'm sure they will be glad to see you."

Winifred said she would like to
stay very much, as she was rather
hungry, so the two ducks waddled
hopefully up to the farm.

"Hello, Walter," called Mrs Smiles. "Have you brought a friend home to dinner? There is plenty here for both of you." And she put down a big dish of mash in front of Walter and Winifred.

When it was all gone, two full and happy ducks went to sleep side by side on the bank of the river.

Winifred woke first. She
stretched her neck and she
stretched her wings, and she
wished that she could always stay
at Blackberry Farm. But no one
had asked her to stay, so she felt
that she ought to try and find her
way back to her own farm.

When Walter woke she told him that she must go. "Oh, please, no!" quacked Walter. "I am sometimes a very lonely duck here, and I would love you to stay with me always. I'm sure Mr and Mrs Smiles would not mind."

"Oh, Walter dear," sighed Winifred. "That would be lovely." And she told him that she was not very happy at her own farm because the dog there liked to chase her. "You will be all right here," Walter told her. "Our dog Rusty is kind to ducks, and I will stay near you always."

So Winifred stayed at Blackberry
Farm, and Walter was very proud
and very happy to share his house
with her. And they planned one
day to have a family of little ducks
who would love Blackberry Farm
as much as they did.